leisure & culture DUNDEE

Working in Partnership

GLITTERFIES THE GALA

created by

JAY ALBEE

raintree

Capstone company — publishers for children

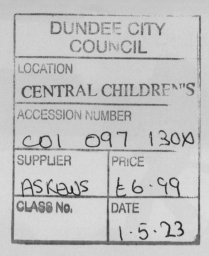
Raintree is an imprint of Capstone Global Library Limited, a company
incorporated in England and Wales having its registered office at 264 Banbury
Road, Oxford, OX2 7DY – Registered company number: 6695582

www.raintree.co.uk
myorders@raintree.co.uk

ISBN 978 1 3982 4898 4

Designed by Nathan Gassman

British Library Cataloguing in Publication Data
A full catalogue record for this book is available from the British Library.

Special thanks to Manu Shadow Velasco for their consultation.

Printed and bound in India.

CONTENTS

I'M RILEY!

I LOVE SO MANY THINGS! I LOVE CRAFTING.

THE ONLY THING BETTER THAN MAKING A MESS IS MAKING COOL STUFF.

I LOVE MY PARENTS, MY COUSINS AND MY FRIENDS.

I LOVE DOGS AND CATS . . .

AND BIRDS AND FISH . . .

AND DRAGONS AND UNICORNS AND ALL ANIMALS!

I'M NON-BINARY, AND I LOVE THAT TOO. I DON'T HAVE TO BE A BOY OR A GIRL.

I CAN JUST BE ME!

MX AUDE TEACHES HELPFUL TERMS

Cisgender: Cisgender (or cis) people identify with the gender written on their birth certificate. They are usually boys or girls.

Gender identity: Regardless of the gender written on a person's birth certificate, they decide their gender identity. It might change over time. A person's interests, clothes and behaviour might be traditionally associated with their gender identity, or they might not.

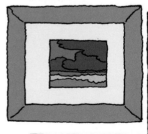

Title: Young people use titles when they talk to or about adults, especially teachers. Mr is the title for a man, Mrs or Ms for a woman, and Mx is the gender-neutral title often used for non-binary people. It is pronounced "mix". Non-binary people may also use Mr, Mrs or Ms as well.

LGBTQ+: This stands for lesbian, gay, bisexual (also pansexual), transgender, queer. There are lots of ways people describe their gender and attraction. These are just a few of those ways. The + sign means that there are many, many more, and they are all included in the acronym LGBTQ+.

Non-binary: Non-binary people have a gender identity other than boy or girl. They may be neither, both, a combination or sometimes one and sometimes the other.

Pronouns: Pronouns are how people refer to themselves and others (she/her, they/them, he/him, etc.). Pronouns often line up with gender identity (especially for cis people), but not always. It's best to ask a person what pronouns they like to use.

Queer: An umbrella term for people who identify as LGBTQ+.

Transgender: Transgender (or trans) people do not identify with the gender listed on their birth certificate. They might identify as the other binary gender, both genders or another gender identity.

CHAPTER ONE

A PROFESSIONAL FESTOONER

The library where Mum worked was a small local branch. It was an old three-storey building, wedged between a dry cleaner's and a tiny park.

The library wasn't usually open on Sundays, but Mum, Riley and Dad had been there since the morning. They were prepping for a party that night.

The library was having a fundraising gala with food and drinks and stuff to buy at a silent auction. A silent auction is where people write down what they will pay for something without seeing how much anybody else has written down. The highest bid wins. It can be very exciting!

The big item for the silent auction was Dad's painting for the cover of the next Throne of Flame and Truth book. The book was called *Allegra and the Dragon*. The books were written by famous, private author L. L. Lamar. Dad did all the covers. When Dad painted this one, he had got Riley to wear a crown and hold a sword so he could take reference photos. Now the painting stood propped up on a table in the middle of the library. It looked spectacular! Riley was sure it would raise loads of money.

Riley had made decorations to match the theme of the painting. There were paper flags, shimmery green dragon scales and golden jewels. Crêpe paper streamers hung from the banisters, bookshelves and door handles.

Riley hung extra streamers and paper stars on the closed lift doors. They thought the lift should be absolutely covered in decorations – or festooned. *Festooned* was a word Riley had heard recently. And that's how they wanted the lift doors to look.

Everyone needed to remember that the whole reason for the gala was to raise enough money to fix the broken lift. Riley made a sign that said: OUT OF ORDER (so please donate!)

Riley stepped back from their work on the lift and smiled. They were happy with how festooned it was. It was definitely the first thing that people would see when they arrived. Then Riley wondered if the most festooned thing should be the *Allegra and the Dragon* painting. Should *that* be the first thing that people saw when they arrived so they remembered to bid in the auction? Before Riley could decide, their best friends Lea and Cricket arrived with Lea's mum. They were going to help set up for the gala too.

"Riley!" Lea called from the door. "The lift looks so good!"

"And look at your dad's painting!" added Cricket. "Wow!"

Riley beamed. Question answered: everything was just right.

OUT OF ORDER
So PLEASE DONATE!!

CHAPTER TWO

THAT'S ONE WAY TO AVOID AN OVERDUE FINE

Lea and Cricket had arrived just in time. Riley had run out of things to do. And Paola was going to arrive soon. Paola was the other librarian at this branch. Riley really did not want to see her today.

Lea's mum carried a big shopping bag to where Mum was setting up another table, just to the side of Dad's painting. Lea's mum had brought a dozen adorable dragons of different sizes that she had knitted or crocheted. They would be in the auction too.

"Did you make any of those dragons, Lea?" asked Riley.

Lea gave Riley a look like "have we met?" and shook her head, laughing.

"Mum made most of them on the sidelines of my games and practices over the last few weeks."

"They look great!" said Cricket. "I know my stepmum will bid on some for sure."

Cricket had four younger half-siblings, and they would love the dragon toys.

Lea looked around. "You know, it feels weird being in the library when it's closed."

"I was thinking the same thing," agreed Cricket.

"It does?" asked Riley.

They looked around too. Riley was here all the time when the library was closed. They went with their dad when he picked up Mum after work. They would wait around for her to finish working.

Riley tried to imagine what it would be like if they'd never seen the library like this – quiet and empty and with only half the lights on.

"Yeah, it's like seeing a teacher at the supermarket," laughed Lea.

"Or seeing your local area on the news," added Cricket.

Riley laughed. "I get that," they said.

Just then, Paola came into the library, pushing a trolley full of fizzy drinks and champagne.

"The library looks great!" she said as she bustled in. "Oh, you decided to set up the tables like that? I was thinking a slight angle might have more *pop*." She did a "pop" motion with her hands.

Mum had been working with Paola a long time and knew that Paola could spend hours on getting the angle of the table just right. But Mum had been planning this gala for weeks, and she'd been working hard all day. Riley knew when Mum was in business mode, no one could change her focus – not even Paola.

Mum said, "Maybe we can think about that later? First we need to set up the drinks tables, get the cash box ready and hang up these other items for the auction."

"Right!" said Paola, with the full force of her enthusiasm. "I'm on it! Just a few more loads to come in from my boot! Oh, hi, Riley!"

Riley waved at Paola and quickly tugged Lea and Cricket towards the stairs at the back of the room.

"Come on, I'll show you some of the out-of-bounds stuff."

"Amazing," breathed Lea, kind of nervously, following Riley as they dashed up the half-lit stairs to the next floor.

"Hold on," Cricket said once he'd caught up. "What just happened? Are you avoiding Paola?"

"Ugh," Riley said. "No. Maybe. Okay, yes, I am." Riley sighed. "I've got an overdue library book, and I don't want to get into trouble."

"Oof," said Lea. "Paola is so intense about overdue books."

"Right?" agreed Riley.

"Once she threatened to suspend my library card," said Lea.

"Why don't you just return it?" asked Cricket.

"I can't find it!" Riley said. "And I'm out of renewals."

"Ah," said Lea and Cricket together.

"I've just got to avoid her until I find the book. It has to be somewhere. Anyway, come and check this out," said Riley, leading Lea and Cricket through the shelving stacks to a closed door.

"Riley, this door says 'Employees Only,'" whispered Lea. "We're not supposed to go in here."

"I know," Riley whispered back and opened the door.

CHAPTER THREE

EMPLOYEES ONLY IN THE LIBRARY OF THINGS

"What is this place?" asked Lea.

"It's the Library of Things," replied Riley, smiling.

"Woah," said Lea and Cricket.

They stepped into the room. It was as neatly organized as the rest of the library, but all the shelves and cubby holes were full of things instead of books.

Riley explained, "It's stuff that isn't books that you can borrow from the library."

In the kitchen section, Lea held up a hook-shaped attachment for a stand mixer.

"What's this?" she asked.

"What does the label say?" asked Riley.

"Um, 'dough hook'." Lea looked at the dough hook. "But what does it do?"

"Who knows!" said Riley. "I don't know what half this stuff is!"

Lea picked up the next item on the shelf and read, "Sausage-making attachment."

"Ooh," said Riley. "I've never seen that one! It's always booked out." Riley looked over the white plastic funnel with a short tube on the end.

From another part of the room, Cricket said, "Hey! We can use this green screen for our explorers project! We can climb a mountain and dive under the sea!"

Cricket was making the *beep boop* sounds he made when he was excited. "*Boop boop!* This will be so much fun!"

"What's the last thing you borrowed from here?" Lea asked Riley. "There's so much to choose from!"

Riley pointed out a briefcase of polished leather with shining clasps. "I carried my paint set around in it for a week." Lea and Cricket laughed.

The friends ran around the cramped stacks shouting out what they were finding:

"A bubble machine!"

"Fourteen wigs! No, fifteen!"

"Ice-cream maker!"

"Ukulele! Accordion! Bongos! Kazoo!"

"A human skeleton? What?!"

"It's a plastic cast," Riley said. "I promise it's not a real one. I checked."

"Oh," said Cricket, a little disappointed.

"Hey," said Lea. "Check this out!"

Cricket and Riley rushed to Lea. Cricket said, "*Beep boop beep!*"

Lea had found a tape player, huge and silver. There was a box of cassette tapes in the cubby hole too.

Riley grinned wide. "Just what every party needs."

Suddenly, the door to the Library of Things burst open.

"Ah, Riley, here you are," said Paola from the doorway. Riley gulped.

"Oh, hi, Paola," said Riley.

Paola said, "Riley, I –"

"Sorry, Paola, can't talk. I've got to take this stuff to Mum." Riley, Lea and Cricket bustled past Paola, who held the door open for them.

CHAPTER FOUR

WHAT'S A PARTY WITHOUT MUSIC?

Riley and their friends took their findings downstairs. The drinks table had been set up, ready to sell to a crowd. At least, they hoped it would be a crowd.

The library really needed a lift that didn't trap people inside it once a week. And it wasn't right that the people who got trapped the most were the ones who couldn't make it up and down the stairs.

On a big whiteboard, Dad had drawn a border in erasable market pen. Vines were intertwined with flowers, little dragons, crowns and swords. Mum and Lea's mum were taping sealed envelopes to it. Some of the envelopes had the name of what was inside, like a voucher to a local restaurant, a promise that Dad would paint a pet portrait, or a week of free classes at the yoga centre.

Some of the envelopes just had question marks on them. People would bid on them in the silent auction without knowing what they were or what they were worth. Riley had some money to bid on a mystery prize. What if it was a pony ride, free pizza for a month or a bright green frog in its very own terrarium?

"Dad! Mum! Look what we found!" Riley yelled.

Dad grinned at the discovery.

Mum laughed and hugged Riley. "Amazing. What's a party without music?"

"That's what I said," said Riley.

"Are you three staying out of trouble?" asked Lea's mum.

"Yep," they all replied, and it wasn't even a lie, really.

Dad flipped through the tapes. "Holy cats," he said, "there are some solid gold tunes in here. Let's get this party started!"

He slipped a tape into the player and

winked at Mum. As soon as the first notes filled the room, Mum smiled wide. Riley did too. This was one of Mum's favourites. She danced every time she heard it. Now she put her hands in the air and flicked her hips. In the next moment, everyone was dancing along.

When the next song started, Mum, still dancing, went back to taping up envelopes. Riley saw that Mum was still focused, but with every beat, business mode was melting away. She turned to Riley, Lea and Cricket. "Can you three run downstairs and grab napkins and cups?"

"Sure, Mum."

"Posthaste!" added Mum.

Posthaste was a funny thing Mum said when she meant "right now" but wasn't cross about it. Riley bounced down the basement steps with Lea and Cricket close behind.

When Mum was dancing, the party was definitely started!

CHAPTER FIVE

DOWNSTAIRS IS WHERE THEY KEEP THE NAPKINS, CUPS AND GHOSTS

Downstairs was a storage area. There were windows high up that showed people's feet as they walked past the library, and, best of all, the dogs they were walking.

Riley flicked the light switch but only one light came on. That happened all the time. The next library fundraiser should be to fix the downstairs wiring.

Riley didn't like coming down here alone. There was something spooky about the way the concrete stayed so cold. And it was so quiet. They were glad to have Cricket and Lea there with them.

"Come on," said Riley. "Everything is in the cupboard over here."

Cricket followed Riley into the gloomy cellar. Lea stayed at the base of the stairs, in the light spilling down from the floor above. She said, "Actually, I'm going to stay here. I'm a bit scared of the dark. Not, like, afraid of it. But not *not* afraid, either."

"There's nothing to worry about," said Cricket.

"I know that," replied Lea, "but knowing that doesn't change how I feel."

"It's okay, Lea," said Riley. "Stay there. We'll throw the packet of napkins to you!"

Lea laughed. "Okay!"

At the cupboard, Riley passed piles of cups to Cricket. Riley picked up a packet of napkins and was about to throw it across the cellar to Lea, when they heard Lea yelp in fright followed by a second, squeakier yelp.

"Lea!" called Riley, rushing back to the stairs. "Are you okay?"

There, Riley and Cricket found Lea – and Nelle. Nelle was a shy younger girl, and Riley's neighbour. The second yelp had come from Nelle!

Nelle gulped and said, "Your parents said you were down here, and I came to help." Being shy, she had moved quietly. Lea didn't know she was there until Nelle touched Lea's arm. Now, Nelle and Lea shook with laughter.

"You okay?" asked Riley, who couldn't really tell if the shock was wearing off or sinking in.

"Yeah," gasped Lea, "I think so." She took Nelle's hand, and they laughed even harder.

"Here, take these." Riley handed Nelle a package of napkins and Lea two piles of cups from their overloaded arms.

Then Mum's voice came down the stairs. "Riley, have you got those cups?"

"Coming, Mum!" Riley shouted. They all dashed up the stairs.

CHAPTER SIX

THE PEOPLE MAKE THE PARTY

Cricket and Lea took the cups out and put them out as fast as Paola could pour drinks. There were already dozens of grown-ups filling the tiny library space and more coming in through the doors.

Lea's mum was taking money and calling out drink orders. Riley didn't know how much it cost to fix a lift, but they were definitely on their way!

"Thanks, kids!" said Paola. "And Riley, don't go home tonight before I get a chance to talk to you, okay?"

"Okay," Riley said as they ducked away.

They found Mum and Dad, supervising the silent auction. The auction was really busy, which was brilliant. And some people were already making song requests at the music station.

"Mum, do you need anything else?" Riley asked.

Mum gave Riley a quick hug, "Thanks, Ry. Go and grab me a snack, will you?"

"I'll help," said Nelle, who was still by Riley's elbow.

Riley and Nelle shuffled and squeezed through the crowd. The party didn't have a dress code, but Riley could tell that people had made an effort. It was a beautiful evening. There was art and drinks, and the party was called a gala! If that didn't make it feel special and worth putting on fancy clothes, then Riley didn't know what would.

Outside, Nelle's mum and dad were selling snacks from their food truck. They were donating all the money they made that night to the lift repair. Nelle and Riley stood in the queue. The queue was long but moving quickly. They talked about which mystery envelope seemed like it might have the most interesting prize. Soon enough they were at the front.

"Riley!" Nelle's mom beamed. "How's it all going inside?"

"Good, I think. There are lots of people," Riley said.

"Lots," agreed Nelle, who could get nervous in crowds.

"Stick with me, Nelle, and let me know if you need to go somewhere quiet for a bit. I know all the best spots," Riley said.

"Thanks, Riley," said Nelle.

"Three tacos, please."

"And one for me," added Nelle. She never got sick of her parents' tacos. Riley took out some money, but Nelle's dad waved it away.

"Tonight, you eat for free!" he said. Nelle's mum handed Riley two samosas and a cookie as well.

"Thanks, Mr and Mrs Jackson," said Riley, then headed back inside.

"Thanks, Ry," said Mum and Dad when Riley handed over the snacks. "You can share the rest with your friends."

Riley picked the mystery envelope they wanted to bid on and Mum carefully wrote the envelope's number down. Then Riley and Nelle went to find Lea and Cricket.

On the way through the crowd, Riley found their neighbour, Toby. Toby was a grandma who had been trapped in the lift last week. She was a huge fan of the Throne of Flame and Truth series and told Riley the story of every book just right, because Riley was too young to read them yet.

She was standing in front of the painting, soaking in all its details.

"I just want to stand here and look at this painting until the next book comes out," Toby said with a happy sigh.

CHAPTER SEVEN

SAMOSAS AND SECRET STRANGERS

Lea and Cricket were sitting on the stairs to the second floor, where they had a view of the whole party. Riley and Nelle sat down next to them. Cricket's stomach rumbled.

He looked at Nelle's snacks and said, "Wow, that smells good."

Riley handed him a samosa, "Dairy-free vegetarian for you."

They handed Lea a cookie, "Gluten-free for you."

Then, taking a big bite, Riley said, "And yummy for me."

Over happy, steaming bites, the friends looked out over the party. The room was so full that the door had to be propped open and the party spilled out onto the pavement. The smell of the Jacksons' good food wafted in on the warm night air.

"Now the library feels even more different," said Lea.

Riley realized she was right. They had always felt that even when it was empty the library was full of life. It was full of stories and facts and stuff like dough hooks and briefcases. But now the library was filled with chatting and laughing and music.

"And, I mean, we're not usually allowed to eat in here."

"Yeah," agreed Riley. "It's great."

"Look, there's Mx Aude and Mr Lane," said Cricket, pointing out their teacher and school librarian.

"It's weird seeing your teachers all dressed up at the library!" laughed Lea.

Riley saw Dad, trapped in a corner by Paola. Riley knew what she was asking him about. Paola was sure that Dad knew the plot of the next Throne of Flame and Truth book, even though he didn't.

Dad pointed out another person in the crowd, who was wearing a nice jacket and standing near Riley. Riley watched Paola push her way through the crowd towards the stranger. She stuck out her hand and started talking immediately.

"Hello! I'm Paola. I was just talking to my friend about the Throne of Flame and Truth series. He does the cover art for it, like the painting there with the dragon and Allegra and the mountain. It's my favourite series! My friend said that you were the person to talk to about it," Paola said.

After a moment, Riley decided that Paola had meant the stranger was the person to talk *at* about it. The stranger couldn't get a word in.

Eventually, Paola had to pause for a breath, and the stranger said quickly, "It was so nice to meet you, Paola. I just have to do something . . . excuse me," and slipped away into the crowd. Riley chuckled. It looked like they weren't the only one avoiding Paola tonight!

Riley watched as the stranger made eye contact with Dad across the room. The stranger made a pretend angry face and Dad winked. Huh, so Dad knew the stranger. Riley wondered who he was.

CHAPTER EIGHT

MYSTERY (ENVELOPES) SOLVED

Soon it was time for the auction winners to be announced. Dad stopped the music so Mum could read out the winners. People cheered when they won a voucher envelope or knew someone who had. There was lots of cheering. Cricket's stepmum won four of Lea's mum's knitted dragons.

They were going to do the mystery envelopes last, and Riley was nervous-excited. But first, the big *Allegra and the Dragon* painting.

"The highest bidder for this very special artwork is . . ." Mum checked her list and called out, "Lew Lamar!"

The whole room – and those peeking in through the open door – gasped.

Lea, Cricket and Nelle asked, "Who's Lew Lamar?"

"L. L. Lamar! He's the writer. The author. He writes the Throne of Flame and Truth series!" whispered Riley.

If Lea, Cricket and Nelle reacted, it was lost in the hubbub of the room. The room was loud with astonishment and guesses about who might be the famous writer.

Mum waved her hands around and Dad did his loudest whistle to quieten everyone down. "Lew has a few words."

Then the stranger in the nice jacket who had been cornered by Paola stepped up next to Dad and faced the room. The audience clapped and cheered.

"Thank you," Lew Lamar said. "It is my great and humble honour to donate the painting to this library, for everyone to enjoy."

But that wasn't all. Lew Lamar was pleased to announce that all the mystery envelopes were prizes that he had donated – things like signed books, voicemail messages and even a lunch. The crowd erupted into gasps of excitement, even as Riley let out a sigh of disappointment. Not a pony ride or free pizza or a frog after all. They didn't even really mind when someone else won the envelope they had bid for. The winner, Mr Bamber from a few streets away, was thrilled with his prize.

Mum announced that they had raised enough money to fix the lift. Everyone cheered, Dad turned the music up again and the whole room became a dance floor.

Soon enough, all the snacks were eaten, all the drinks were gone and all the dances were danced. What a night! The only people left were the clean-up crew: Mum, Dad, Riley, Lea, Cricket and Paola.

Riley, Cricket and Lea filled big black bags with napkins, cups and crêpe paper streamers for the recycling collection. Riley always tried to keep a bag and one of their friends between themself and Paola. But being vigilant was tiring, and it had been a long day. Riley only let their guard down for a second.

"I've been trying to catch you all night!" said Paola, standing right next to Riley.

Riley was taking the streamers and stars off the lift. There was nowhere to hide!

Riley sighed, slumped a little and said, "Oh, Paola. I'm sorry! I know, I know. *The Age of the Dinosaurs* is overdue and I'm out of renewals. I'll bring it back soon, I promise!"

Paola looked surprised for a moment, then confused.

Cricket said, "That's the book you've been worried about? Riley, you lent it to me last time I was at your house. I brought it back to the library days ago. On time!" Cricket laughed.

"I did?" asked Riley. "You did?" Cricket nodded.

Riley's face brightened, "Oh! Okay then!" Riley looked at Paola. "I'm so relieved! If I don't have an overdue library book, what did you want to talk to me about?"

"I wanted to ask if you would teach me how to make these stars you hung on the lift," said Paola. "My son is getting engaged and I think these would be wonderful decorations for his party!"

Riley laughed, more at themself than anything that was actually funny, and said, "Of course, Paola, that sounds fun."

In no time, Mum and Paola agreed that the library was clean. Riley proudly added one more sign to the lift, smiled and headed home. What a night!

THE END

DISCUSSION QUESTIONS

1. Why do you think it's so important to fix the lift in the library?

2. Riley avoids Paola because they don't want to get in trouble for an overdue library book. Was this a good way for Riley to solve their problem? Why or why not?

3. Do you think the gala was a good idea for a fundraiser? What kind of fundraiser would you like to go to?

WRITING PROMPTS

1. Pretend that you won a mystery envelope at the silent auction. Write about what you got and how you feel about it.

2. Everyone has fears. Lea is a bit scared of the dark. What are you scared of? Write a list of things you can do to face one of your fears.

3. Pretend you get to stay overnight in the library for a night. Write about your adventure.

MEET THE CREATORS

Jay Albee is the joint pen name for LGBTQ+ couple Jen Breach and J. Anthony. Between them they've done lots of jobs: archaeologist, illustrator, ticket taker and bagel baker, but now they write and draw all day long in their row house in South Philadelphia, USA.

At a party, you'll find Jen and J. out on the dance floor.

Jen Breach

J. Anthony